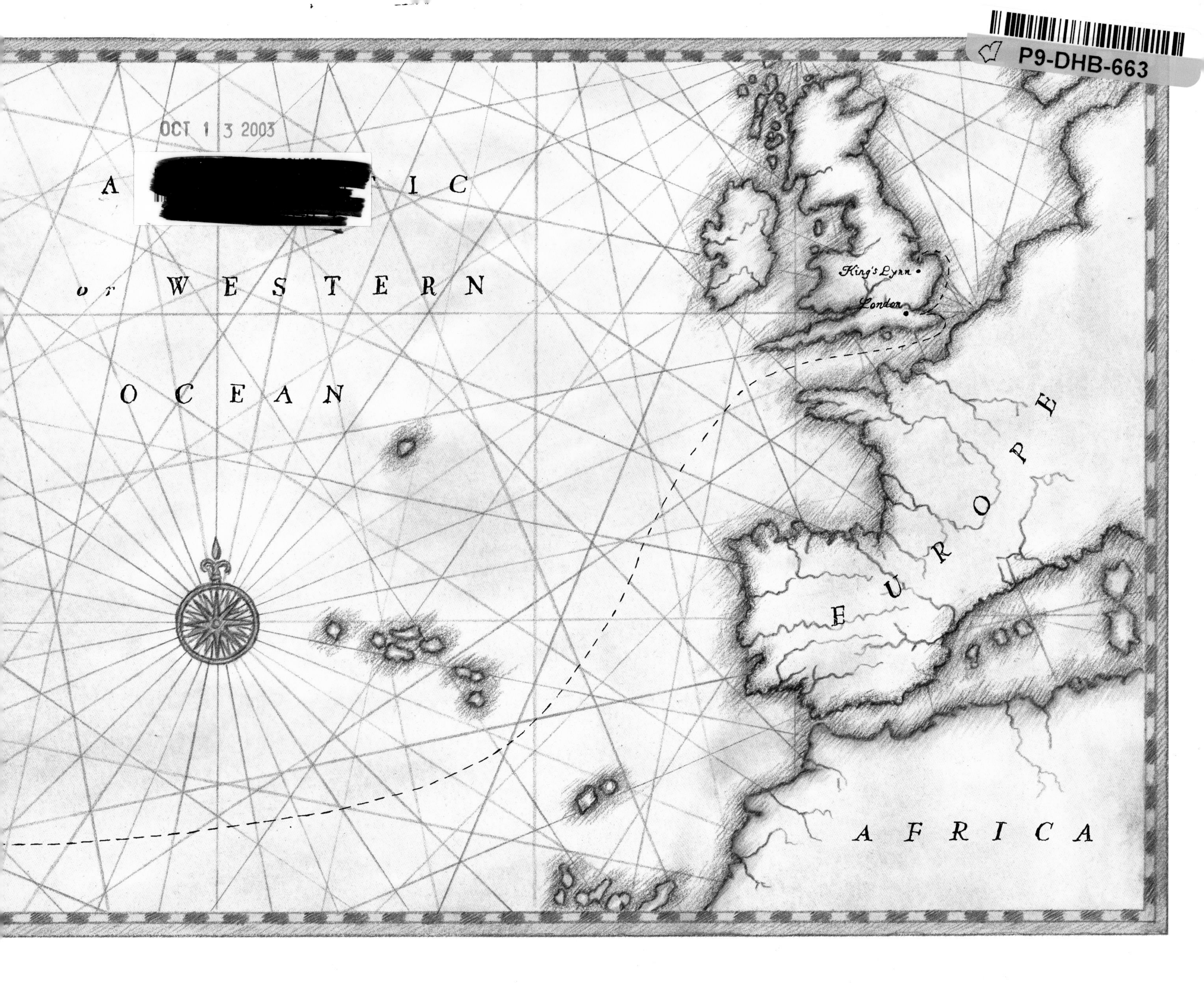
or WESTERN
OCEAN
King's Lynn
London
EUROPE
AFRICA

A *TALEWINDS* Book
First published in the United States of America in 2002 by:
Charlesbridge Publishing
85 Main Street
Watertown, MA 02472
(617) 926-0329
www.charlesbridge.com

Library of Congress Cataloging-in-Publication data is available upon request.

Printed in Singapore
(hc) 10 9 8 7 6 5 4 3 2 1

The Lucky Sovereign was edited, designed, and produced by
Frances Lincoln Limited, 4 Torriano Mews, Torriano Avenue, London, U.K. NW5 2RZ

The LUCKY SOVEREIGN

Stewart Lees

TALEWINDS
A Charlesbridge Imprint

Sam watched, spellbound, as his father carefully tipped shiny gold coins into a leather pouch.

"That's twenty-five gold sovereigns," he said proudly.

"Are we rich now, Pa?" whispered Sam.

His father smiled at him. "No, not rich," he said, gripping the bag tightly. "But I've enough saved here to buy all the land we can manage in this new colony they call America."

"Then you won't have to work these fields for Squire Trelawney anymore, Pa."

"It's what your mother and I always dreamed of, Sam—our own land. I wish she had lived to see it. Next month, we sail!"

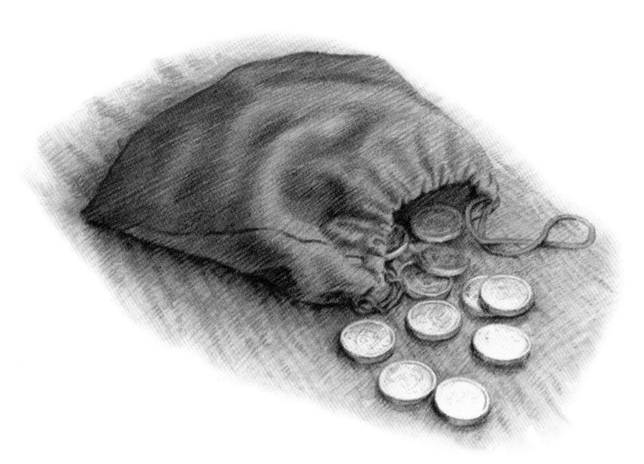

It was dark when they set off. Old Jed, their neighbor, had offered to take them to the coast in his wagon. They left the silent fields and by midday were in the noisy, bustling port of King's Lynn. Merchants and traders thronged the busy quayside, and Sam soon found himself gazing up wide-eyed at the wooden sides of their ship, the *Treasurer*.

Suddenly Jed turned and pressed a coin into the boy's hand. "Take it," he said. "This sovereign saved my life at the Battle of Cadiz. It was in my breast pocket and stopped a Spanish musket ball that was heading straight for my heart."

"Oh Jed! Thank you," said Sam. He passed the coin to his father. "Put it with the others, Pa. Perhaps it will bring us luck."

On board the crowded ship, Sam and his father stood watching the teeming dockside below. They spotted Old Jed, who raised his hat and waved.

Then the great sails were unfurled and caught the wind. There was a loud cheer as ropes were untied and the *Treasurer* began to slip slowly out of port.

They sailed steadily around the southern coast of England. The crew, some not much older than Sam, scampered over the rigging without fear. With only the swaying lantern light to guide them, they worked into the night preparing the *Treasurer* for its long, perilous journey to the New World and the small settlement of Jamestown.

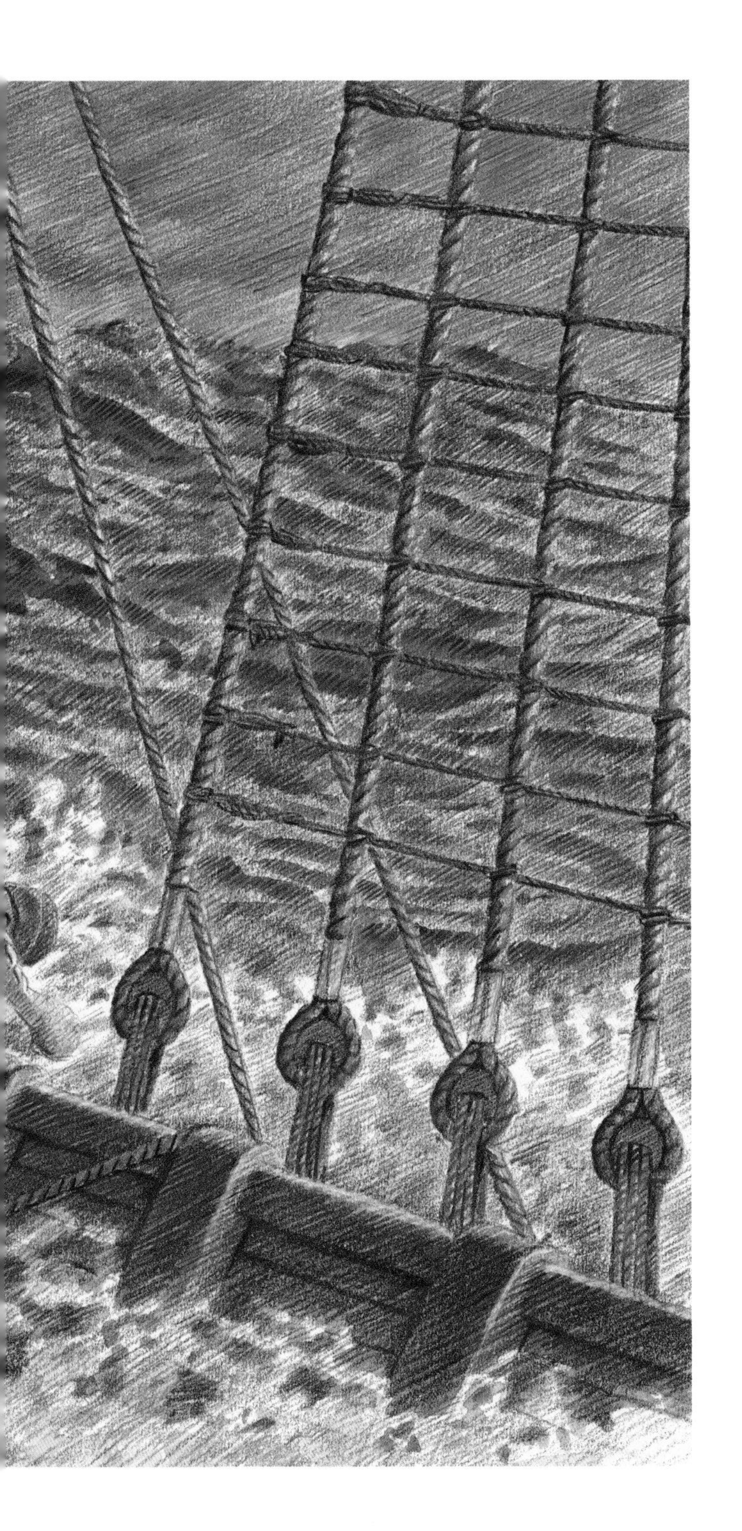

The captain set a southwesterly course through calm, warm waters. Dolphins swooped playfully through the bow wave ahead of the ship. But as it headed due west out into the Atlantic Ocean, the dolphins disappeared.

Then a terrible storm lashed and shook the *Treasurer*—a storm so fierce that two men were swept overboard. A third was crushed horribly by shifting cargo. Sam stood silently with the crew the next day as the man's body was wrapped in sailcloth and sent over the side to join his crewmates.

As the youngest on board, Sam kept out of everyone's way by helping Tom, the ship's cook, down in the galley. The crew's diet was poor. Without fresh fruit or vegetables, many men began to look ill and feverish. But Tom let Sam have a few extra rations in return for his help, so neither Sam nor his father fell sick.

One day, Tom wanted a sack of flour, so Sam went down the rickety stairs to the storeroom. He braced himself for the usual scuffling of rats fleeing into the shadows, but this time heavier sounds made him stop. He heard something fall onto the wooden deck, followed by the sound of a man cursing under his breath. Sam turned and fled back up the stairs, locked the door behind him, and ran to find Tom.

"There's someone in the storeroom!" he said breathlessly. "I've locked him in."

"I had a feeling we had a thief on board," said Tom. "Now, thanks to you, we've got him!"

The next afternoon, the whole ship's company assembled on deck as the thief—a crew member known as Flint—was brought up from below, escorted by the lieutenant and the first mate.

The flogging that followed was brutal and bloody. When it was over, Flint was led away. As he passed, Sam looked up and was met with such an evil, piercing glare that his blood turned to ice. He knew that he had made an enemy.

As the days grew warmer, the crew seemed happier. And when one day there came a shout of "Land ho!" from the lookout in the crow's nest, the men stopped what they were doing and cheered and whooped at the top of their voices.

Everyone crowded on deck to get a first glimpse of the New World. As evening fell, the *Treasurer* dropped anchor next to a flat, marshy headland at the mouth of the James River. At first light the ship would sail the final thirty miles upriver to Jamestown.

Sam lay on his bunk that night savoring the stillness. The ship's timbers creaked gently, and the waves slapped lazily against the side. From the deck above, he could make out muffled sounds: voices, laughter, and music.

Curious, Sam climbed the ladder and slowly opened the hatch. Laughing, shouting, and singing filled the warm night air, and through it wove the sound of accordions and whistles, clapping and stomping. Sam noticed his father nearby, somehow managing to sleep through it all.

Then a movement in the shadows next to his father caught his eye, and Sam tensed as a familiar figure emerged—Flint!

Before Sam could cry out, Flint stood up, looked nervously around, and melted away into the shadows.

Sam, wake up!" Sam sat up in his bunk. It was morning. "Something terrible has happened." His father's face was white, his eyes frightened. "Our sovereigns are gone!"

While his father went off to search the deck once more, Sam sat on his bunk, his mind racing. *Flint!* he thought. But how could he report what he'd seen? He shuddered at what Flint might do to him if he got him into trouble again.

The door burst open. It was Tom. "Sam! Flint told the Jamestown governor that your pa's got no money, and now your pa's under arrest. You know what that means: they'll put him to work as a slave!"

Sam gasped and quickly told Tom what he'd seen on deck the previous night.

"Listen, Sam," said Tom. "There's a fellow in Jamestown called John Rolfe. I knew his father back in Norfolk. When we go ashore, we'll look him up and see if he can help."

The next day Flint, Sam, and his father stood facing the governor of Jamestown. Next to him sat John Rolfe. The bag of coins sat in the center of the governor's desk. Sam had told his story, and now Flint stepped forward.

"They do spin a wonderful yarn, Your Honor," he said, "but rest assured, this scoundrel and his lying son have landed here with not a penny between them."

This was too much for Sam. "My pa's not penniless!" he shouted. "He's got twenty-five gold sovereigns he saved—and my lucky sovereign!"

John Rolfe leaned forward. "What lucky sovereign?" he asked. Sam told him about Old Jed and the coin that had saved his life.

"Then surely, Governor," said Rolfe, "if this bag truly belongs to Sam's father, it must contain the lucky sovereign."

The governor tipped out the bag of coins and turned each one over carefully. Sam held his breath as the governor lifted one of the sovereigns up to the light.

"Well, bless my soul," he said. "Just look at that." And there, in the middle of the coin, was the unmistakable dent of a musket ball.

Sam and his father stood watching as the *Treasurer* slipped her moorings to begin the long voyage back to England. Weeks earlier they had watched Flint being led away in irons. Now they were saying goodbye to Tom, who was going back with the *Treasurer*.

John Rolfe was also leaving, returning to London to do business on behalf of the colony. He stood on the ship's deck with his beautiful young wife, Pocahontas, and their baby son, Thomas. Tom joined them, and they all waved to Sam and his father as the ship moved slowly out into the river.

"D'you know, Pa," Sam said, "I never really looked at that sovereign when Jed gave it to me."

"To tell you the truth," said his father, smiling, "Old Jed's been telling that story ever since I was a boy, and I never believed a word of it."

Sam looked down at the gold coin glinting in his palm. "Do you think it will bring us luck here in Jamestown?"

"Yes, Sam," his father said, squeezing Sam's hand. "It will. It already has."

JAMESTOWN

Sam and his father would have arrived in Jamestown, Virginia, the first permanent English settlement in America, in 1616. Jamestown was founded nearly ten years earlier on the shores of the Chesapeake Bay by Captain Newport. Under the leadership of Captain John Smith, the settlement survived many hardships.

Legend has it that Smith himself survived an early encounter with Native Americans of the Powhatan Confederacy only after the dramatic intervention of Pocahontas, the daughter of Chief Powhatan. And it is also said that when John Smith later had to return to England, the young girl was heartbroken.

It was another son of Norfolk, John Rolfe, who introduced tobacco as a cash crop, helping the colony toward economic success. In 1614 he fell in love with and married Pocahontas, thus securing peace with her people.

In this story Sam witnessed John Rolfe and his family setting sail for England. Sadly, Pocahontas died on the eve of their return voyage, and Rolfe returned to Virginia alone. Their son, Thomas, remained in England until he was an adult, then returned to Virginia and married. Today, many Virginians can claim direct descent from John Rolfe and his Native American bride, Pocahontas.

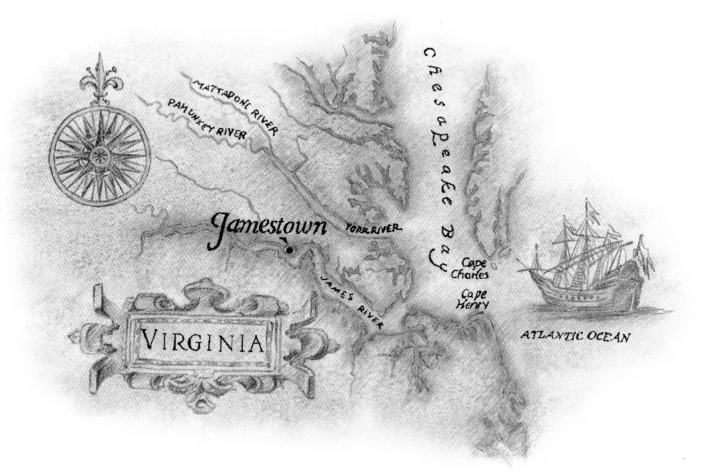

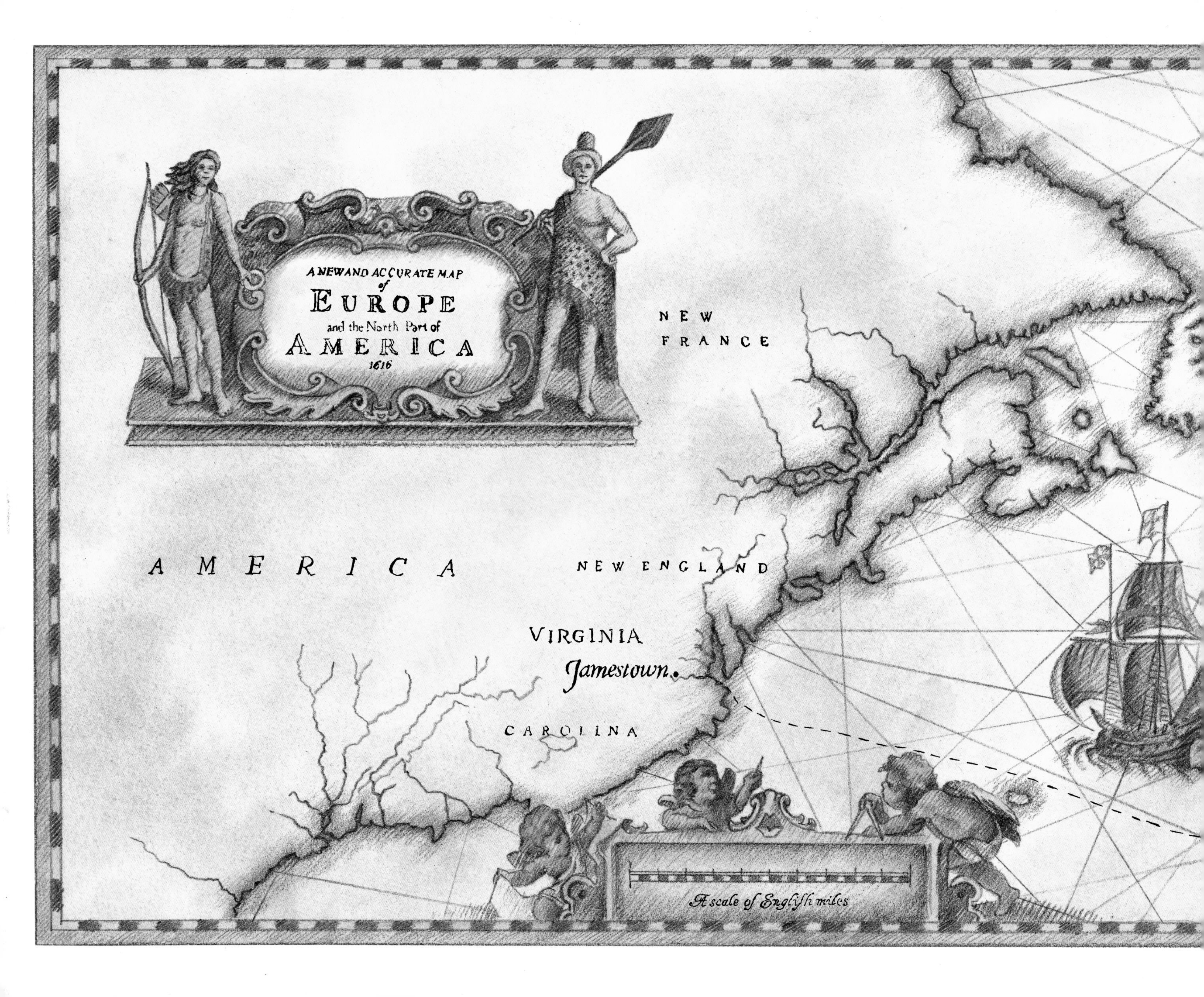
A NEW AND ACCURATE MAP
of
EUROPE
and the North Part of
AMERICA
1616
NEW
FRANCE
AMERICA
NEW ENGLAND
VIRGINIA
Jamestown.
CAROLINA
A scale of Englysh miles